BENEATH THE BLOCKS

AN UNOFFICIAL MINECRAFTER MYSTERIES SERIES

BOOK TWO

BENEATH THE BLOCKS
AN UNOFFICIAL MINECRAFTER MYSTERIES SERIES
BOOK TWO

Winter Morgan

Sky Pony Press
New York

Copyright © 2018 by Hollan Publishing, Inc.

Minecraft® is a registered trademark of Notch Development AB.

The Minecraft game is copyright © Mojang AB.

Sky Pony Press books may be purchased in bulk at special discounts for sales promotion, corporate gifts, fund-raising, or educational purposes. Special editions can also be created to specifications. For details, contact the Special Sales Department, Sky Pony Press, 307 West 36th Street, 11th Floor, New York, NY 10018 or info@skyhorsepublishing.com.

Sky Pony® is a registered trademark of Skyhorse Publishing, Inc.®, a Delaware corporation.

Minecraft® is a registered trademark of Notch Development AB.
The Minecraft game is copyright © Mojang AB.

Visit our website at www.skyponypress.com.

10 9 8 7 6 5 4 3 2 1

Library of Congress Cataloging-in-Publication Data is available on file.

Cover design by Brian Peterson
Cover art by Megan Miller

Print ISBN: 978-1-5107-3188-2
Ebook ISBN: 978-1-5107-3194-3

Printed in Canada

TABLE OF CONTENTS

BENEATH THE BLOCKS

1

GREAT NEWS

"That's amazing!" Edison exclaimed to Omar.

"What's so amazing?" Billy overheard them. They were standing at Edison's potion stand in the center of town.

"Omar is building a castle in Verdant Valley," Edison blurted out.

Billy didn't find this to be amazing news. "Oh no, you're leaving Farmer's Bay?" he asked.

"Just for a few months," Omar reassured Billy. "I won't be gone long, and you can visit me."

Edison reasoned, "He's only moving one town over. It's a quick trip. It will also give us an excuse to visit Anna."

Billy looked down at the ground when he spoke. "I know you're right, Edison." He looked at Omar. "I want to apologize. I realize you told me something really great, and I immediately thought about myself."

"You don't need to apologize. I'm flattered that you care about me moving to Verdant Valley." Omar smiled.

"Tell us about the castle," Billy said. "Will you build a moat?"

"Yes." Omar described the castle in great detail as Billy and Edison listened attentively.

"What made you decide to do this?" asked Billy.

"I was asked to build it," Omar replied.

"By whom?" Edison questioned.

"It's a rather odd story, but a few days ago I went to the village to trade some of my wheat for emeralds, and I encountered a cloaked man named Dante."

"A cloaked man?" asked Edison.

"Yes, Dante wore an orange cloak, and he asked me if I knew who had built the mansion by the water. Dante told me that he was living on a boat and had seen the mansion from the water and was instantly drawn to the structure. I told him that it was my home, and he immediately offered me countless diamonds for the building. I was taken aback because nobody has ever offered me a large sum of diamonds for anything I have ever built. There was a part of me that wanted to sell my home and take the diamonds, but I remembered that I love my home and never want to sell it. I explained that the home wasn't for sale, but Dante wasn't happy with this news.

"I told him that I could build him a home, and he suggested that I craft a large castle. I agreed. I didn't hear from Dante for a few weeks, but yesterday he knocked on my door and told me that he acquired a bunch of land in Verdant Valley and asked if I was available to start constructing the castle. I told him I could start this week."

"So you aren't moving there?" asked Billy.

"Dante wants the castle built very quickly, so I'm afraid I will be staying in Verdant Valley until the project is complete," said Omar.

Edison wanted to tell his friends about the great news in his life. He had run out of ghast tears for his potions, and he traveled to the Nether on his own and was able to refill his supply of rare ghast tears. The trip wasn't easy, and there were many times when he thought he'd be obliterated by a ghast or a blaze, but he had made it home in one piece, and he was quite pleased with the outcome. However, this news seemed rather minor compared to Omar's.

"I have ghast tears," Edison told his friends, "so I have to go home and start finishing a bunch of potions I was unable to brew before."

"Wow," Omar remarked, "ghast tears are hard to get."

"Yes." Edison told them about the trip to the Nether.

"Next time," Billy said, annoyed, "can you ask me to go with you? I heard about a great Nether fortress I want to loot."

Edison agreed he'd tell Billy about his next trip to the Nether, but Omar interrupted as he looked up at the sky, "It's almost dusk. I have to get to Verdant Valley before night. I want to get an early start on Dante's castle. Anna said I could stay at her house tonight."

Omar turned around and waved as he left the town ready to start building Dante's castle.

Billy asked Edison if he needed help closing up for the night. Edison was a respected alchemist and sold his potions at a stand in the village in Farmer's Bay. People came to visit his stand from all across the Overworld. As they placed the final bottle of potion into the case, a woman with long dark hair and glasses called out, "Can you just wait one second?" She rushed over, and catching her breath she asked, "Do you have any more potions for breathing underwater?"

Edison looked through his inventory and found one bottle of the potion of Water Breathing. "Only have one. Do you want it?"

"Yes," she said, "I'm so glad you have even one. I'm not a very good alchemist, and I've been in dire need of this potion. How much does it cost?"

"One emerald." Edison held the potion as the woman picked an emerald from her inventory.

"Thank you," she said. "You have no idea how helpful this is to me."

"I don't mean to pry," said Edison, "but it's very late. Where are you from? How are you going to get home before dusk?"

The woman pointed to the sea. "I live on a boat. Don't you see it docked at the edge of town?"

Edison and Billy looked over at the beach and saw a large pirate ship in the water. Billy asked, "Wow! That's incredible. That's your boat?"

"Yes." She blushed. "I built it. I'm a huge fan of

pirate stories, and I've always wanted to live on a pirate ship."

Edison said, "Me too. I love pirate ships."

"If you'd like to go on the boat, I am staying here overnight, and I'd be more than happy to give you a tour of the boat tomorrow."

"Can I come too?" asked Billy.

"Of course," she replied, and then she added, "I'm Amira."

Billy and Edison shook her hand as they introduced themselves. Amira smiled and excused herself. "I have to get back to the boat before nightfall."

The two friends also had to get home before night. They didn't want to fight off the hostile mobs that spawned in the darkness. As the two cleaned up and raced back to their bungalows, an arrow pierced Edison's unarmored shoulder.

"Ouch!" he called out.

Four skeletons aimed their arrows at them. Edison put down his case and pulled out potions and threw them at the bony beasts. Dousing the skeletons with potion weakened them, and Billy slayed the skeletons with his enchanted diamond sword. One by one, Billy destroyed the beasts, and they dropped bones and an arrow.

"We did it!" Edison smiled as he picked up one of the dropped bones. "Let's go home before anything else happens."

Kaboom!

"I think it might be too late," Billy said as he regained his balance after the explosion.

"What was that?" asked Edison.

Smoke billowed from the shoreline.

"Amira's boat!" they exclaimed in unison.

2

PIRATE SHIP

"We have to help Amira!" instructed Edison. "We can't! It's nighttime—we have to wait until morning," said Billy. "If we leave now we're going to be incredibly vulnerable to hostile mobs. Besides, we don't really know Amira at all."

The night sky camouflaged the dark smoke. Edison stood in front of his bungalow, stared into the darkness, and said, "We have to go. There was an explosion in our town. We have to find out what happened, but I should leave my case in my house. If we get destroyed, I don't want to lose all of my potions."

Peyton and Erin raced out of their homes. Peyton asked, "What was the explosion?"

Erin held onto her torch as she looked toward the sea. "It sounded like it was coming from the shore."

"We think a ship exploded," said Billy.

"The pirate ship?" asked Peyton.

"We think so," said Billy.

Edison quickly placed the case of potions on the floor of his small living room, closed the door behind him, and hurried toward his friends when he spotted zombies lumbering in the darkness.

"Turn around!" Edison hollered.

"Oh no!" Billy cried when he felt a zombie grab his shoulder. He held his breath to avoid feeling sick from the odor of rotting flesh.

Peyton and Erin weren't dressed in armor, and the zombies pulled at their arms as all four friends tried to grab diamond swords from their inventories. Billy readjusted his armor and raced to the zombies. Edison sprinted after Billy. He clutched a bottle of potion in one hand and an enchanted diamond sword in the other, and as he ran he splashed the undead creatures with potion.

Erin fumbled with her diamond sword, accidently dropping it on the ground. She tried to fight the zombie that attacked her while she picked up the sword, but the zombie was too powerful. With each strike, her hearts depleted until she respawned in her bed.

Peyton swung her diamond sword at the zombie that destroyed Erin. Slamming the sword into the fetid-smelling beast, she annihilated the zombie. Another zombie lurked behind Peyton, but she swiftly battled the zombie until it was also destroyed.

"Peyton!" Erin emerged from her house with a replenished health bar. She was dressed in armor and ready to battle any undead mob that spawned in the thick of the night.

Edison and Billy were in the midst of their personal battle against three zombies. Both struck the smelly zombies with their diamond swords. When the final zombie was destroyed, Edison picked up the rotten flesh they dropped on the blocky ground and said, "We have to race to the shore."

They hurtled past the town farm, and a familiar voice called out in the distance, "Edison! Billy! Help me!"

"Amira!" Edison screamed.

"We're over here!" Billy called out.

Peyton asked, "Who is Amira?"

"She's the person who lives on the pirate ship," explained Billy. "We met her today when she bought a potion of Water Breathing from Edison."

Amira followed the sound of their voices and reached the farm. Tears streamed down her face. "It was awful." She could barely speak.

"I know you're upset, but you're going to have to take a deep breath," Billy said calmly.

Edison suggested everyone head to his house, where they could talk safely. "There are zombies spawning all over here. It will be easier to talk in my house."

The gang crowded in Edison's tiny living room, and Amira spoke, "I was about to go on my ship when it exploded. Who would do that to me? I am just an explorer, I'm not someone who loots others' treasures."

Edison asked, "I know you say that you're just an explorer, but can you think of anybody who might be a suspect? We should have a list."

"Wow, you sound like a detective," Amira said as she paced the living room trying to come up with any potential suspects. "Are you one?"

"I'm not a detective," Edison replied.

"We did solve the mystery surrounding a string of robberies in town," said Billy. "Edison, our friend Anna, who lives in Verdant Valley, and I did it together. It wasn't easy, but we did it."

Peyton wanted to change the subject and remarked, "You did a good job with that, but we have to concentrate on Amira's pirate ship. I was admiring it earlier today. I can't believe somebody destroyed it."

"I've been traveling around in that boat for over a year. I've explored all of the shore towns."

"All by yourself?" asked Erin.

Amira paused before she replied, "Yes." Edison found the pause slightly suspicious and made a note of it.

"Wow, that sounds lonely," remarked Peyton.

"It's not." Amira brushed her dark hair from her face. "I don't mind being by myself. Some might call me a loner."

"Well, if you don't mind some company," said Edison, "you can stay here until you rebuild your boat."

"Thanks," Amira smiled, "That's so nice of you."

Edison wanted Amira to stay in his house so he could keep a close eye on her; there was something about Amira that he didn't trust. He recalled how she paused when he asked her if she was alone on the boat. He wondered if she was telling the truth. He was also a fan of pirate stories, but he knew that pirates weren't good people. Maybe Amira wasn't just a fan of pirates, but was also a lone pirate who traveled from port to port, plundering villages. At the moment, she was his only suspect. Perhaps she had blown up her own boat? There were many questions, and Edison wanted answers.

Peyton yawned. "I think I have to go back home. I need to sleep."

Erin said, "Me too. Let's all walk out together. It's safer if we stick together."

Billy, Peyton, and Erin walked into the dark night while Edison showed Amira her new room.

"I can't thank you enough for doing this for me," Amira said, and she climbed into bed.

Edison was too nervous to sleep. He hoped that Amira wouldn't rob him while he slept. After he finally closed his eyes, he awoke to the sound of thunder. He rushed to the window to see the rain pattering on the glass. It was morning and the ground was muddy, and he noticed footprints on the ground. The footprints belonged to a wild ocelot that raced around his property. He looked through his inventory for fish to tame the ocelot. Once he picked fish from his inventory, he opened the door and put his hand out for the feral ocelot. It raced into the dry doorway. Leaning over his hand, the ocelot smelled the fish and took its first bite. The wild ocelot transformed in a tamed cat, and Edison invited this new pet into his home. The cat rubbed against Edison, and he spoke to the animal. "I think I'm going to call you Puddles, since I discovered you in a puddle."

Puddles explored his new home, peeking his head into Amira's room. Edison followed the ocelot and called out, "Amira, my new pet wants to say hi."

There was no reply. Edison looked in the room. The bed was made and the room was empty. Amira was gone.

3
RAINY DAY

"Amira!" Edison walked out into the rainy morning, but there was no reply. Puddles stared at Edison from the doorway. The rain soaked through Edison's sneakers, making each step uncomfortable as he searched his yard. He wanted to go back inside and dry off, but he had to find Amira. Edison walked down the sandy path leading to the shorefront. The remnants of the charred boat barely clinging to the shore were in eyeshot. He hoped to find Amira assessing the damage to her ship, but she wasn't anywhere to be found. Instead, Edison spotted three skeletons in the distance. He pulled armor and a bottle of potion from his inventory. The three skeletons outnumbered him, and he considered hurrying back to his bungalow to shield himself from bony beasts, but he didn't have the time. The skeletons raced toward Edison, and he had no choice but confront his enemies.

One of the skeletons shot an arrow, and Edison jumped out of the way to avoid being struck. As he lunged at the skeletons, ready to douse them with potion, he was startled to find all three skeletons outfitted in enchanted armor. Armored skeletons were very rare, and Edison knew this battle wasn't going to end well. Battling three normal skeletons was challenging, but trying to annihilate three armored skeletons was next to impossible. Due to the armor, the potions had no effect on the skeletons, and they had the energy to unleash a powerful barrage of arrows that instantly destroyed Edison.

Edison respawned in his bed, rubbed his eyes, and got up. The rain had stopped. Puddles stood by the door. Edison had stopped to pet the ocelot when Billy walked in.

"Crazy rainstorm, right?" he asked Edison. "I woke up with four zombies tearing down my door. What a morning. I'm so glad that's over."

"Amira is missing," Edison announced.

"No she isn't. I saw her walking with Erin."

"Really? She didn't tell me she was leaving." Edison was both annoyed and relieved.

"They were walking to her pirate ship. I think it's in very bad shape. Should we go see it?" asked Billy.

Edison nodded his head and followed Billy to the ship. The sun was shining, and he could see Amira and Erin standing on the beach, looking at the boat.

Billy sprinted to Amira, "Do you think you can rebuild the boat?"

"Yes." Amira pointed to the gaping hole in the front of the ship and the burnt sails. "Before I started on my life at sea, I was a builder. I can probably rebuild the ship in a week or so."

"You can stay with me until the boat is complete," offered Edison.

"Thank you, Edison." Amira beamed as she spoke. "That's so helpful. I know you're a fan of pirate stories, so if you have any ideas for the new design for the boat, I'd love to hear them."

Edison blushed. He loved the idea of helping Amira with the boat, but he also wanted to maintain his distance from her. He couldn't become her friend when she was his primary suspect.

"I'd love to help," Edison replied.

"Great, I'm going to get started now. I don't want to have to stay with you forever," she laughed.

Erin and Billy were also eager to help Amira construct the boat. Amira said with a smile, "I feel so incredibly lucky to have had my boat destroyed in Farmer's Bay. I've never met such a nice group of people in my life."

"Maybe if you didn't spend all of your time alone at sea, you'd see that people are usually very nice," said Billy.

Amira shook her head. "That's not usually the case. Before I left for my life at sea, I encountered a lot of people who weren't very nice." Amira didn't expand on this comment. She just stood and stared at the sky as if she was recalling something in her memory that she didn't want to share with the others.

Edison said, "Well, I don't know what happened to you in the past, but I can assure you that our town has some the nicest people in the Overworld."

Edison wanted to know Amira's backstory. He wondered if the people who bothered her in the past might have walked into the present. However, he knew from the last case that he solved that these things take time, and it was better to observe and take notes than to jump to any conclusions.

Amira walked to the boat, her ankles were covered in water, and tried to climb up the burnt ladder. But she fell down. "I think we should start with crafting a new ladder."

Erin gathered sticks to construct a ladder. "You know, we have an incredible builder who lives in our town. If he we ask him to help us, I bet we'll finish this really quickly."

"Are you talking about Omar?" questioned Billy.

"Yes," Erin replied as she placed the sticks on the ground to form the ladder.

Billy explained, "Omar is living in Verdant Valley for a little while."

"What? Why?" asked Erin.

"He was asked to build a castle in Verdant Valley," answered Edison.

"Wow," said Erin.

"And it's going to have a moat and everything," added Billy.

"Wow, that sounds exciting," said Erin.

"Later today, I was hoping to go over and see

what he's doing. Would you like to go with me?" asked Billy.

"Yes," said Erin.

"Great." Billy then asked Edison if he wanted to join them.

Edison paused before he replied. He wanted to see Omar, but he also wanted to keep a closer eye on Amira.

"Who asked him to build the castle?" asked Erin.

"Some guy in an orange cloak," Billy said as he finished the ladder.

Amira rushed over. "Did you just say an orange cloak?"

"Yes," said Billy.

Erin smiled proudly. "We finished the ladder. Let's carry it over to the boat and climb abroad."

Amira didn't even thank them for the crafting the ladder. Instead she asked, "Did your friend Omar happen to mention the name of the man who asked him to build the castle?"

"Yes," Billy said. "Dante."

Amira sighed, and Edison took note. He wondered if she knew someone in an orange cloak and if that was the person from the past who had bothered her.

4

ALL ABOARD

Amira finally thanked them for work they did on the ladder.

"This ladder is perfect," she remarked.

The group carefully carried the ladder to the burnt ship and leaned it against the side.

"You should be the first one on the boat," said Edison.

Amira climbed up the ladder. Before Edison, who was trailing closely behind her, was able to climb onto the boat, he heard Amira unleash a loud, pain-filled cry. When he got onto the boat, he saw her weeping next to a row of burnt chests.

Tears streamed down her face. "Not only is the boat damaged, but I also lost everything I ever owned."

"Do you have anything in your inventory?" asked Edison.

"Yes," she sniffled, "but not much."

"We'll help you replenish," Billy said, and Erin agreed.

Edison was shocked that Billy offered up all of them to help. He wasn't ready to give Amira goods to refill her chests. He happened to be running low on resources, and he didn't want to give them to a person he viewed as a suspect.

Amira led them through the pirate ship, and with each step she'd tell them to be mindful of the burnt planks. She didn't want them falling through the planks to the deck below. Amira repeated, "I can't believe somebody would do this to my boat," as she walked across the boat's deck.

Edison walked very slowly, taking note of everything. He figured the boat would be teaming with clues to help him solve the case. He had to inspect it carefully. Whoever wanted to destroy Amira's pirate ship had to have been aboard the ship to place the TNT in the middle of the boat.

The large hole where the TNT had been placed was covered in soot. Edison looked down the hall and leaned over to get a closer look. "I think the person only used two bricks of TNT. I bet they weren't trying to destroy the pirate ship, but were definitely sending a message."

"A message?" Amira was confused.

"What type of message?" asked Erin.

"It was a warning, I assume," said Edison. "They weren't trying to destroy the ship—they were trying to damage it."

"Do you think they wanted me to stay in this town? I mean, they knew if they destroyed my ship, I wouldn't have any way of leaving," Amira suggested.

Edison agreed with Amira's theory that someone was trapping her in the town. Now he just had to find out who wanted her here.

A voice called out from the shore, "Is there anybody there?"

"Who is that?" Amira grabbed her sword as she rushed to the side of the ship to peek at the shore.

"It sounds like Omar," said Billy.

"Your friend who is building the castle?" Amira asked. Looking down at the beach, she asked, "Who are you?"

"Who are you?" the voice replied.

"I'm Amira."

Edison walked next to Amira. "That's Omar," he told her.

"Edison," Omar called up to them, "what are you doing on a burnt pirate ship?"

"It's a long story," Edison called down to him. "Why don't you come up?"

Omar climbed up the ladder and met them on the ship. "Wow, somebody did a number on this ship. Is it yours?" he asked Amira.

"Yes," she replied. "Your friends are helping me rebuild it. Somebody blew it up yesterday."

"That's awful." Omar inspected the boat. "But this seems like an easy repair. I bet you could finish this in a few days."

"I hope so," said Amira. "I want to go back to my life on the sea."

Omar walked over to the gaping hole in the ship's center. "This will be the hardest repair. I'd love to help you, but I only came back to town to purchase some potions from Edison. I'm in the middle of a big project in Verdant Valley."

"Your friends told me that you're building a castle for a man named Dante."

"Yes, I just started the construction."

Amira told Omar about her previous life as a builder and how she worked on a castle that had a moat. She went into details about the construction of the bridge that ran over the moat.

"You seem to be an expert at building castles," remarked Omar. "I have an idea. If I help you fix your boat, will you help me build my castle?"

"I want to get back to the sea"—Amira paused—"but I guess I can do it. I really enjoyed working on the other castle, so I'm sure this would be fun. Also, there are many things you have to keep in mind when you're building a castle that you only learn once you've built one."

Omar was thrilled. Edison said, "It will be great to have you back in Farmer's Bay, even if it's just for a couple of days."

Amira and Omar walked around, surveying all of the damages and listing what they needed to do in order to fix the boat. They gave everyone a job and a list of items they needed to obtain.

While Edison got his orders from Amira and Omar, he looked out at the village in the distance. He could see a small line standing in the center of the town. "I want to help you guys," Edison said, "but I think I have a line of customers. I have to sell my potions."

Omar said, "I need to buy some too. I will be in the line later."

Amira said, "Edison, you have been so generous to me by letting me stay in your home. If you can't help build the boat, that's okay."

"I will try and help," Edison explained. "I just don't know how much of a help I can be."

"I'm sure you will be very helpful," Amira smiled.

Billy asked Edison if he needed help at the potion stand, and Edison happily accepted.

"Yes, I'd love it," said Edison. It was tough to work alone when there was a large crowd.

Edison and Billy excused themselves and climbed down the ladder to the sandy shore. They were just a few steps from the ship when they heard a loud horn.

"What's that?" Billy turned around and said, "Oh my!"

Edison's eyes widened as a large yacht sailed toward the shore. Billy pointed to the lavish boat. "I wonder who is on this boat."

5

PORT OF CALL

Edison and Billy waited at the shore. This wasn't an easy decision—he knew there was a line at the potion stand—but they both wanted to know who was on the yacht that was inching its way toward the shores of Farmer's Bay. Omar, Amira, and Erin climbed down the ladder.

Omar raced to the yacht. As it docked, Omar climbed aboard the boat. Edison walked to Amira and Erin and asked, "Is that Dante's boat?"

"Yes," Erin said. "Dante is here to discuss the plans for the castle."

Edison was curious to see how Amira interacted with Dante. He wouldn't have to wait long, because Omar called to them, "Hop aboard."

The gang walked up the yacht's ladder and onto its glitzy deck. "Wow," Billy whispered to Edison. "This boat is so fancy, it has a swimming pool."

The swimming pool in the center of the deck wasn't the only amenity. The boat also had many lounge chairs with umbrellas and a kitchen. The multilayered yacht was so large that Edison couldn't believe it was seaworthy.

Dante introduced himself. "I've come to your beautiful town because I was told one of the best builders in the Overworld lived there. Once I met Omar, I knew it was true."

Dante's yacht had a higher view, and Edison spotted a very long line at his potion stand. He was torn and didn't know if he should stay abroad the yacht or serve his customers.

Dante offered to give them a tour of the yacht. The gang walked around each floor, looking in all of the rooms.

Billy said, "You have so many rooms, I think you could house all of the people from our town on this boat."

"Are you the only one who lives on the boat?" asked Edison.

"It's me and my staff," said Dante.

The second he spit out the word *staff*, a man dressed in a tuxedo and a bow tie walked over. "Did you call for me?"

"No, Gregson," Dante said, "but now that you're here, I'd like to introduce you to Omar and his friends. This is Gregson; he's my butler. Everyone, will you please introduce yourselves?"

Edison watched Amira closely. She didn't seem to

be fearful of Dante or his butler, and he felt that there weren't any more clues to be found aboard the yacht, so he excused himself. Billy reluctantly joined Edison. He wouldn't say anything, but he was upset that he wasn't able to spend more time aboard the yacht. Billy had never been anywhere that nice, and he wished he could have spent the day swimming in the pool and relaxing on the spacious deck.

When Edison finally arrived at the potion stand, the first customer remarked, "You have no idea how long I've been standing here."

Another asked, "Where were you, Edison? You think I have all day to wait for you?"

A man in a blue jumpsuit said, "This better not happen again, or we're going to start buying our potions from someone else."

Edison felt bad. He apologized and explained, "My friend's boat was damaged by TNT, and we had to help her fix it."

"That's awful," a customer remarked.

Edison tried to keep the line moving along, but it was hard to manage the crowd. He had a handful of customers left as the sun began to set. Billy took orders and payments as Edison pulled the potions from the inventory. As the sun set, they finished with their last customer.

"Omar never showed," said Edison.

"We can't wait for him, because it's too dark." Billy looked at the sky.

As the sky grew darker, the duo readied themselves

for an attack from hostile mobs by suiting up in armor and placing the rest of the potions in their inventories. Edison and Billy clutched their diamond swords as they walked back to their bungalows.

"I really hope we can make it home without being attacked," said Edison.

"Me too," Billy said, but he paused when he saw two block-carrying Endermen walking past them.

They stood still, trying not to make eye contact with the lanky Endermen, but Billy must have stared at one of them, because it made a high-pitched sound and teleported toward him.

Billy and Edison narrowly avoided being destroyed by the Endermen as they ran as fast as they could toward the shore. Edison let out a sigh of relief when he felt the water on his feet and knew he was safe. The Endermen chased them into the water and were instantly obliterated.

The friends dried themselves off on the sandy beach. Edison's sneakers were drenched, and he took them off for the walk home. The pair was on the lookout for hostile mobs as they cautiously trekked across the beach.

Billy pointed to the shore. "Look, there's Amira. Should we ask her if she wants to walk back to the bungalow with us?"

Before they had a chance to talk to Amira, she pulled a bottle of potion from her inventory, took a large gulp, and jumped into the water. Seconds later, Dante climbed down from his boat, sipped a potion, and jumped into the sea.

"That's strange," remarked Edison.

"Do you have any potion of Water Breathing?" asked Billy.

"No," Edison said. "I sold my last bottle to Amira yesterday. I didn't have any time to brew a new batch."

"Let's go back to your house and brew some," suggested Billy, and the two raced through the town in the dark night.

6

WATER BREATHING

"**W**e're almost there," Billy said as they bolted past the farm.

"But we're not safe!" Edison screamed, and he raced toward a group of foul-smelling zombies who were ripping the doors from the hinges of Peyton and Erin's homes.

"Help!" Erin cried while she plunged a sword into the oozing flesh of the undead beast.

Edison splashed a potion. As the zombie lost more hearts, Erin delivered the final blow.

"Look behind you!" she warned Edison while picking up the pieces of rotten flesh the zombie had left behind.

Three more zombies lumbered toward Edison. He pulled out a bottle of potion, but it was empty. He slammed his enchanted diamond sword into one of the zombies, slicing into its flesh. Even though he was able to destroy it, he had lost too many hearts in the battle and didn't have the energy to fight the remaining zombies. Even with Erin at his side, he was weakened to a point of exhaustion, and when he felt a zombie's grimy hand on his shoulder, he knew it was over. Edison respawned in his bed. Puddles meowed, but he didn't have time to pet the cat. He raced out the door, ready to help his friends, but the zombies were gone.

Edison called for them, but there was no response. He walked back to his home, but he wasn't ready for bed. He went over to his brewing stand and started working on a batch of potion of Water Breathing. He had taken out a bottle, some Nether wart, and a pufferfish and started to brew the potion when his door opened. He assumed it was Billy, because they had discussed brewing the potion in order to see what Amira and Dante were doing underneath the sea.

"Billy?" Edison called out from behind his brewing stand.

"No," the voice called back. "It's Amira."

"Really? I thought you were Billy."

"What are you doing up so late?" she asked.

"I didn't have time to work today. I have to brew my potions for tomorrow's crowd. They were very upset that I was late today," Edison babbled. He didn't want Amira knowing that he was brewing a potion of Water Breathing to follow her.

"That's my fault," she apologized.

"No, it isn't," Edison said. "I wanted to help you."

Amira walked over to the potion stand and stared

at all of the ingredients he had out. "Wow, you really work hard. I never knew an alchemist's job was this difficult." She yawned.

"I think there is a difficult aspect to every job," Edison replied as he quickly bottled the potion so she wouldn't see what he had brewed. He placed the bottles in his case and started to brew a batch of potion of Invisibility.

"I have some good news," said Amira.

"What is it?" Edison asked as he placed a fermented spider eye into the potion.

"Dante is staying in town for a few days. He is letting me stay on his boat. You can have your place back to yourself."

Edison didn't think this was good news. He wanted to Amira to be close by so he could keep an eye on her.

"That's great." He rubbed his eyes. Edison could barely stay awake, but he did have a bunch of potions that needed replenishing, and he had to fill orders for the morning crowd.

"I'm also going to help Omar with the castle. Once the boat is repaired, I'll be staying in Verdant Valley."

"I thought you wanted to be alone on your boat and you didn't like staying on land," said Edison.

"I do, but I'm beginning to like it here," she said, and then she wished him a good night and went into her room.

He tried to brew the remaining potions, but he was getting tired, and after a few batches, he was literally falling asleep standing up. He didn't want to brew a weak batch, so he went to bed. In the morning, the sun was shining, and Billy knocked on the door.

"I can help you today," said Billy.

Edison got his potions together. As they walked into town, Edison updated his friend about Amira's moving to the yacht and staying on to help Omar.

"Wow," said Billy. "I bet Amira and Dante are working together."

"They might be," said Edison, "but it doesn't make any sense. Why would Amira destroy her own boat?"

"I don't know," said Billy, "but tonight we should see if they jump into the water again. Don't sell all of your potions of Water Breathing. Just set two aside for us."

When they reached town, there were a couple of people waiting in the line, but it was nothing compared to the previous day's crowd. Nobody complained when they arrived. Edison set up his stand and opened for business. One of Edison's first customers of the day was a familiar face.

Dante, dressed in his orange cloak, remarked, "Looks like you have a good business here. You must brew very strong potions."

Edison blushed. "I'm one of the only alchemists in the area."

"I'd like to purchase some potions." Dante listed a few, but only one stood out in particular. "I'd like two bottles of the potion of Water Breathing."

"You're in luck," Edison said. "We have only two left."

"Can I put an order in for tomorrow?" asked Dante.

"Of course. A lot of my customers do that," said Edison.

"I'd like twelve bottles of Water Breathing," said Dante.

"Twelve bottles?"

"Yes. Can you do that?"

Billy looked at Edison. "That's a lot of bottles. I can help you."

"Yes, I can do it," said Edison.

Dante pulled out a pile of emeralds and handed them to Edison, "I'd like to pay you in advance."

Edison placed the emeralds in his inventory.

"Can you deliver them to my ship tomorrow morning?"

"Of course," Edison said, although he wasn't sure he had all of the ingredients for the potions.

"Good," Dante smiled and walked away.

"Twelve bottles," said Billy. "What does he need twelve bottles for?"

"I don't know, but we're going to find out."

Edison packed up his potions for the day. Billy helped Edison carry the case as they walked back to the bungalow. They were exhausted from a day of selling potions, and they replenished their energy with a cake and apples.

"I'm concerned I might not have all of the ingredients to brew twelve bottles of potion," Edison confessed.

"Let's see if you do," said Billy. "I'll check my inventory, too."

The duo scanned their inventories, and they had just enough supplies to brew twelve bottles of the potion of Water Breathing.

"Thankfully, we don't have to sell Dante our two bottles," Edison remarked.

"I know," said Billy. "Now we need them more than ever. We have to see what he's doing under the sea."

They stopped talking when Amira walked in.

"I hope you don't mind if I stay here," said Amira.

"I thought you were staying with Dante," said Edison.

"I think he changed his mind," Amira replied. "I went there today and he asked me why I was there. He didn't even remember meeting me. It was so strange."

"That is strange," said Billy.

"It's fine if you stay here. Did you get a lot of work done on your boat today?" asked Edison.

"Yes, Omar helped a lot. I wonder if Dante is annoyed at me because I am delaying work on the castle. But he knows I worked on castles before and that I will definitely help Omar complete the castle more quickly than he anticipated."

Listening to Amira, Edison realized she might not be his major suspect anymore. He was going to focus on Dante. He wanted to figure out why he needed twelve bottles of potion of Water Breathing and how he had forgotten who Amira was when he had met her the day before. He had a lot of investigating to do, but now he had to brew twelve bottles of potion. It was going to be a long night.

7
THE DELIVERY

When the last potion was brewed, Edison put the twelve bottles in a separate case to bring to Dante and fell asleep. It seemed like he had barely closed his eyes when the morning sun shone through his window, and he could hear Puddles calling out for his morning meal.

"I'll feed Puddles," Amira said as she placed fish on the floor.

Edison picked up the two cases of potion. One was filled with Dante's Water Breathing potion, and the other was for his regular customers.

"Do you need help?" asked Amira. "It seems like you have a lot to carry."

"Thanks, but Billy is going to help me. He should be here soon," said Edison.

"Before you go, can I buy some potions?" asked Amira.

"Okay, what type do you need?" He put the cases down.

"I need as many bottles of Water Breathing potion that you have in your case."

"I'm sorry, but I don't have any left." As Edison answered, the case filled with the Water Breathing potion fell to the ground and opened. Edison quickly grabbed the potions making sure none of them spilled.

Amira raced over to help him. "Isn't this the potion of Water Breathing?" she asked.

"Yes, but—"

Before Edison had a chance to answer, Billy walked in the door. "Oh no, you didn't drop the potions, did you?"

"No, everything is fine." Edison packed the final bottle into the case and stood up.

"Everything isn't fine," Amira raised her voice. "You lied to me."

"No, I didn't. These bottles have already been sold. I didn't lie. I don't have any bottles of Water Breathing that I can sell," explained Edison.

"Oh." Amira apologized and asked, "Can you brew some for me? I'd like to place an order."

"Yes, but I need a few days. I'm out of pufferfish."

"Is that all you need?" asked Amira.

"Yes, and then I can brew the potion."

Amira said, "Then I will go fishing today and will get you a bunch of pufferfish. If you do that, can you brew the potion when you get home?"

"Yes," Edison replied, and then he left with Billy.

Billy took the case of potions for Dante and walked beside him, "You still have the potions for us, right?"

"Yes, I have those in my inventory, and I wasn't going to sell them to Amira," said Edison. The case of potions was hard to carry. He hadn't been sleeping very much, and everything made him tired.

"Good. Tonight we're going to see what's going on under the sea." Billy's voice was upbeat and energetic. There was an excitement to his tone. Unlike Edison, Billy loved a good adventure. He enjoyed solving mysteries, while Edison found pleasure in crafting a strong potion.

Edison felt his shoes fill with sand as he walked on the beach. He stopped and emptied the sand from his shoes before they walked up the ladder and onto Dante's luxurious yacht.

Dante greeted them, "Wonderful! Thank you for brewing the potions so quickly." He opened the case and eyed the twelve bottles, then called out for his butler, "Gregson, please get us all some cake."

Gregson appeared with a tray of cookies, cake, and apples. "Please help yourselves."

Edison didn't know what to eat first because the platter was filled with so many incredibly tasty choices. Billy picked up a slice of cake and ate it. Edison tried to swallow a cookie before he excused himself, "I have to get to my potion stand."

"Do you have a few minutes? I wanted to ask you something," Dante asked as he blocked the way to the ladder.

"Okay," Edison replied. He wondered what Dante wanted to ask him. He had a lot of questions to ask Dante. He wanted to know why he had forgotten who Amira was and why he needed twelve bottles of Water Breathing potion, but he stood silently and listened to Dante. He knew good detectives listened and didn't talk too much. They didn't want to give anything away.

"What happened to your friend Amira?" asked Dante. "I offered her a place to stay, but she never showed up."

Edison didn't know what to say. He paused and walked toward the ladder and finally said, "I don't know." He climbed down the ladder of the boat with Billy.

When they were out of earshot and they were in town and away from Dante's boat, Billy admitted he was confused. "But Amira told us Dante didn't remember who she was. What is going on?"

Edison agreed, "Something suspicious is going on, and I'm not sure what it is or who is telling the truth."

The day at the stand was uneventful, and Billy and Edison spent a lot of the time trying to put the pieces together, but they weren't getting anywhere.

"I still don't think Amira would blow up her own boat," said Billy.

"I know, but we can't talk about it now," Edison said as he saw Amira walking toward them.

Amira was smiling as she pulled six pufferfish from her inventory. "Look what I have for you."

"Wow, you caught six pufferfish," said Edison. "That's impressive."

"After a year at sea, you learn how to catch fish," she said as she handed the fish over. Then she asked, "Is there any way you can brew the potion now? I am going to Verdant Valley soon. I am going to stay with Omar and help him work on the castle."

"What about your boat?" asked Billy. "I thought you were going to fix it with Omar. Weren't you planning on doing that first?"

"We were, but we decided to work on that in a few days. I'm not using it at the moment, so there really is no rush. Omar needs help making the foundation for the castle. It's a two-person job, and I told him I'd love to help. He is digging the blocks away now and I'm already late. So, can you brew the potion now? I'm in a rush."

Edison apologized, "I can't brew the potion until tonight when the stand is closed."

"Really? Can't you do it here?"

"No, I need my brewing stand," he explained.

"Oh well." She brushed the black hair from her face and looked down. "Keep the pufferfish, and I'll come back for the potion tomorrow."

She started to walk away when Edison called out, "Amira! I realized I had two bottles in my inventory. Would you like them?"

"Yes!" Amira raced back and grabbed the two bottles. "This is fantastic. I'm so happy."

"Great," Edison said. "I just need to keep two of the pufferfish to replace my potions."

"That's fair," Amira said as she placed the bottles in her inventory and sprinted toward Verdant Valley.

Billy watched Amira sprint off in the distance. "You have Nether wart, right? I wouldn't want you to have given her our only two bottles."

"Yes, all I needed were the pufferfish. I'll go home and brew our potions, and then we'll go to the shore tonight. We have to see what they're doing down there and figure out what is happening," said Edison.

"Good plan," said Billy. "Tonight we take a night dive into the water."

When Billy spoke, Edison suddenly remembered he was terrified of being underwater. He had only been underwater once, when Billy convinced him to loot an ocean monument, and he was immediately attacked and destroyed by an elder guardian. Edison could recall the painful sting of the laser-eyed fish. Although the memory was still fresh, he had to toss aside his fears to find out what Dante and Amira were planning deep under the sea.

8

RUMBLING

"**A**re you almost done?" Billy was impatient. He wanted to find out what Dante and Amira were doing beneath the ocean, and he didn't want to wait for Edison to finish brewing the batch of potion.

Edison put the Nether wart in the potion. "Yes, just one second. You can't rush me, or I will brew a weak potion. And we want to stay under the water long enough to investigate, right?" Edison asked as he brewed the potion.

Edison didn't want to admit that he was nervous, and that was also slowing him down. He couldn't work as fast as he usually did because his mind kept wandering back to the moment he was stung by an elder guardian. Puddles rubbed against his calves and meowed, which calmed him down. He was almost finished with the potion when the front door opened.

Omar rushed through the front door. He gasped, "We need your help!"

Amira followed closely behind. Edison was shocked to see her. He had imagined Amira underneath the water with Dante—he didn't think she was with Omar working on the castle.

"What's wrong?" Edison asked.

Omar took a deep breath before he said, "There's something rumbling underneath the castle. We finally dug deep enough to start building the foundation for the castle and the moat when there was rumbling underneath the ground."

"Rumbling?" Edison questioned.

"It felt like a mini-earthquake," explained Amira.

"That's strange," said Billy.

Edison looked out the window. "It's getting dark out. I think we should head over there now, before nighttime."

"We could teleport to Anna's house to save time," suggested Omar.

Edison liked that idea. He hadn't seen his friend Anna in a while, and he missed her. He also knew she was instrumental in solving the last case they were involved in, and he hoped she'd be able to help him with this one.

The four friends stood in the center of the living room and they teleported themselves into Anna's home.

"Billy! Edison!" Anna exclaimed. "I feel like I haven't seen you guys in forever."

"Me too," said Edison.

"Have you heard about the rumbling?" asked Billy.

"Yes," Anna replied. "I was there when the ground started to make odd noises. It was so strange. I thought I was going to be sucked in."

Edison stared out Anna's window. "It's already night. It's too late for us to investigate. Why don't we do it first thing in the morning?"

Anna pointed to a new hallway in her home. "I built an extension to my house. I have two extra rooms, so I can house all of you if you'd like to stay here."

Edison wanted to stay as close to Amira as possible. He was hoping he could catch her leaving to go to the shore and jump into the water if she had plans to meet up with Dante. When Anna showed him to his room, he had every intention of staying up all night and listening for Amira's exit, but once he got into the bed, he fell into a deep sleep. Billy woke him in the morning, shaking his arm.

"You have to get up," Billy said.

Anna was standing next to Billy. "It's time to get up. Omar already left to work on the castle."

"Where's Amira?" Edison asked as he got up from the bed and pulled a glass of milk from his inventory to regain his strength. He was upset that he had fallen asleep and that he didn't get to see if Amira had gone underneath the sea.

"I'm right here." She held a bunch of apples. "I was gathering some apples with Anna for us to eat."

"We should get going," Anna told them as she packed her inventory with a pickaxe and other tools needed to investigate the rumbling underneath the blocks.

The group walked through the grassy meadow until they reached the shaded path that led to Dante's castle. There was a large crater.

"Do you see how large this crater is?" Amira said. "We were just starting to put down the foundation when we heard the rumbling."

"Omar," Anna called out. "We're here to help, and we also have a bunch of freshly picked apples."

Amira held her pickaxe as she climbed into the crater. "Omar? Where are you?"

There was no reply.

"Omar?" Edison raised his voice. "Are you here?"

Billy said, "Maybe he went to town to get something."

Anna suggested, "I'll head to town. You guys wait here."

"I'll go to town with you," said Edison.

As Anna and Edison walked to the small village in the heart of Verdant Valley, Edison told Anna everything. He wanted to run everything by her and see what she thought about the situation. Edison went into great detail about Amira's pirate ship exploding. He told her how Dante offered Amira a place to stay, but she never stayed there. Amira kept staying at Edison's house because she claimed Dante didn't remember who she was. He also told Amira about seeing both Dante and Amira jump into the water.

"Wow, Edison," Anna sighed.

"I know," Edison said. "I didn't want to leave anything out. I hope I didn't overwhelm you."

"No, it's good that you gave me all of the information. It will help in solving the case."

Edison smiled. "Good."

Anna paused for a while and then, as she tried to piece together all of the information, said, "I wonder who blew up Amira's boat. Once we figure that out, I'm sure we'll be able to figure out everything else."

"I know you're right," said Edison. He was glad he ran everything by Anna. He was getting confused by all of the other details, but she was right. Once they found out who placed the TNT on Amira's pirate ship, everything else would fall into place. They walked around the town of Verdant Valley, but they didn't see Omar.

"Omar!" they called out his name in unison, but there was no reply.

"Where can he be?" asked Edison.

"We should head back to the construction site. He doesn't seem to be in town," said Anna.

They walked back to the patch of land where they were building Dante's castle, but there was nobody there.

"Omar! Billy! Amira!" Anna called out.

Edison and Anna searched the blocky ground, climbing down into the heart of the crater, but they couldn't find any of their friends at the construction site. As Edison and Anna climbed out of the crater, the ground began to rumble and shake.

Anna cried out, "I'm falling!"

"Hold onto my arm," Edison called down to Anna. She was inches from him, and he knew that he could get her out safely.

"Help!" Anna screamed. Her foot was caught in a hole between two blocks. She could barely grasp Edison's arm and didn't want to fall into the shaky crater.

"You can do it!" Edison called out.

"I'm trying!" Anna said as she clung to Edison's arm. Her foot was stuck, and her leg was deep in the hole.

Edison tried to pull her up, but he was losing his footing due to the moving surface. "I'm going to pull you up. Just hold on," Edison reassured her.

The grassy ground was wobbly beneath Edison's feet, and he tried to hold onto Anna, but he was growing weaker by the second. A potion would help, but he didn't want to risk grabbing one. It was hard enough holding onto Anna with two hands. If he let one go, she might fall into the crater.

"I have to get my foot out." Anna held onto Edison as she wiggled her foot from the hole. "I did it." She used all of her strength to push toward Edison and landed safely on the ground.

Anna looked down at the crater that was shaking violently. "What is happening?" Anna cried out.

Edison looked at the crater in horror. "How are we going to save our friends?"

9
CALL FOR HELP

The rumbling ended and the ground closed, but Anna couldn't stop staring at the hole in the ground.

"We have to go in and save them," Anna cried as she stared at the rubble.

Edison looked down at the once-shaky ground. "I don't think we should go down there. I'm afraid it might start shaking again."

Anna grabbed her pickaxe and started digging into the grassy patch beneath her feet.

"What are you doing?" questioned Edison.

"There has to be something underneath the ground that is causing all of this," she said as droplets of sweat formed above her brow. "And I'm going to find out what it is because I need to find my friends."

"I think there has to be *someone* behind all of this, and I have a feeling I know who it is." Edison stared in the direction of Farmer's Bay.

"Who?" Anna put her pickaxe down.

"We should go see Dante. He's on his ship," said Edison.

"I don't want to leave here without my friends," Anna protested.

"I might be wrong, but I think digging a hole might not be the wisest way to find our friends. If there is someone down there holding them prisoner, they will probably just capture us too. We have to come up with a better plan."

Anna shook her head. She knew what Edison said made sense. "Okay, let's go find Dante and ask him what he's done to our friends."

"We can't let him know that we suspect him," Edison told Anna.

"You're right," Anna reminded herself. "We have to be very strategic in our approach to solving this case."

The duo sprinted back to the shore of Farmer's Bay, but they stopped when they reached the center of the village and a group of people called out to Edison.

"When are you opening your stand?" said a woman wearing a dark baseball hat.

"We've been waiting here all morning," a man in a jean jacket yelled at him.

"This is craziness. You can't just open your stand when you feel like it. You have a job, and you have to be responsible," an older, gray-haired man hollered.

A girl wearing knee-high socks walked over to Edison. "Just give me a bottle of potion of Invisibility."

Edison looked at the line of people and apologized.

"I'm sorry. I don't have my case. My stand isn't going to be open today. I can't sell any potions."

"What about your friend who helps you?" asked one his regular customers. "Why can't he run the stand?"

"That's the reason I can't open the stand. My friend Billy is missing," explained Edison. As he spoke the words, he felt as if he were punched in the chest. Simply stating the fact that Billy was missing made Edison physically ill. He wanted to be reunited with his friend. He didn't want to stand around explaining why he couldn't sell potions to his customers.

Edison excused himself as the group chatted about his friend's disappearance. As he jogged away, he heard someone ask, "Can we help you find him?" Edison didn't turn around.

They were steps from the shore when Anna looked out and questioned, "Where's Dante's boat?"

Edison stood on the sandy beach looking out at an empty shoreline. "I don't know. Where *is* the boat?"

Anna inspected the shore, searching for anything that might help them find out where Dante's boat was. "Are you sure it was docked over here?"

"Yes." Edison was dumbfounded.

Anna walked over to Amira's burnt pirate ship. "Do you think we should climb abroad this boat and see if you find any clues?"

Edison hesitated. He felt strange going on Amira's pirate ship when she wasn't there, but he knew it was vital to their investigation. They had to inspect everything thoroughly and get all of the information to help find their friends. As he stepped up onto the first rung of the ladder, his heart started to beat very fast.

Anna was already on the boat when he reached the final step. She called out, "Over here. I see something."

"What?" asked Edison as he raced toward Anna.

"It's a book." She picked up a tattered book from the bottom of a burnt chest.

"I thought Amira said everything she owned was destroyed." Edison looked over Anna's shoulder as she opened the book.

The pages were wet, and the words were hard to read. Edison watched as Anna flipped through the pages of the book. "All I can make out is the word *orange*," she said. Anna said, "The water and the explosion damaged the book, but it looks like it was a journal."

"Orange?" Edison said. "Dante wears an orange cloak."

"Oh wow," Anna exclaimed. "I wish I could see what else was written on the page, but that's the only word I can see because the rest of the page is destroyed."

Edison told Anna how Amira was nervous when she heard about a person wearing an orange cloak, but once she met Dante, she didn't seem upset at all.

"We have to find Dante," said Anna. "He's our only hope in getting any answers." She looked through the remainder of the pages. "The rest of the book is unreadable."

Edison walked to the edge of the boat and looked

out. He didn't see Dante's ship anywhere. Looking down, he spotted a bubble in the water. He pulled out the two potions of Water Breathing from his inventory.

"I think I know where we might find him," said Edison.

10

DIVING

"We have to go underneath the water." Edison handed a potion of Water Breathing to Anna.

Anna took the potion. "But Dante's boat is gone. Why do you think he's still under the water?"

"I don't, but I know Dante spent some time down there, and Amira did too. I think it's the place we might find any answers," Edison said, and then he took a big gulp of the potion and jumped into the water.

Anna jumped in after Edison, splashing into the deep blue sea. She had never been underwater before and wasn't sure what she'd find.

"This is beautiful," she remarked as she swam alongside Edison.

The water was peaceful, but Edison knew the deeper they swam, the more likely it was they'd encounter a guardian—or even worse, an elder guardian. He wanted to swim back to the surface, but he knew he had to brave.

"What's that?" asked Anna as she pointed to something swimming in the distance.

Edison's heart beat even faster, and he took a deep breath to calm himself down, but it wasn't working. He thought he could see the thing swimming toward them. "It's a guardian. It's a very dangerous fish." He didn't have time to tell Anna about the time he was destroyed by an elder guardian. But he calmed down when he saw the black tentacles move toward him. "It's just a squid. It's fine. A squid won't bother you."

The relief of not having to battle a potentially hostile fish was short-lived. Within seconds they were swimming deeper into the ocean, and then they saw a school of guardians. The spiky fish didn't see them, and Edison called out to Anna, "We have to hide."

Anna agreed, but asked, "Where?"

In the distance Edison saw a lavish ocean prismarine crystal monument. "We have to get inside that ocean monument, but I don't know how we're going to do it without battling the guardians and then the elder guardians."

There wasn't any time to talk about a battle plan, because as Edison spoke, the guardians swam toward them. One of the guardians focused on Anna. It unleashed a purple laser from its singular eye, which then started to turn a blinding yellow.

Anna froze. Edison screamed, "Anna move! The

laser doesn't have any power yet. You have to get out of the way!"

It was too late. The laser struck Anna, and her hearts began to deplete. Edison remembered the painful sting from the guardian and how it radiated throughout his body. He grabbed his bow and arrow and aimed at the guardian's eye. The arrow landed in the center of the eyeball.

"Bull's-eye," Edison said as he shot a second arrow, which damaged the fish's hearts. It took three more arrows to destroy the fish that weakened his friend and left her in pain. The guardian dropped raw fish, which Edison picked up. He could use the fish to feed Puddles. "At least something good can come of this," he said to himself as he pocketed the fish and swam toward Anna with a handful of potions to help her regain her energy.

"Are you in pain?" he asked as he handed her a potion.

She took a tiny sip, "No, I'm feeling better. I just want to get into that ocean monument."

The duo swam, avoiding the school of guardians near the ocean monument. They were almost at the entrance when one of the guardians shot a laser at Edison. He started to panic. He recalled the last time he had been struck.

"Swim away before it hurts you!" Anna called out.

Edison watched the laser change from purple when he swam from the laser and toward the entrance of the monument. "Thanks," he said to Anna.

Anna shielded herself behind the ocean monument's prismarine crystal pillar and shot arrows at the fish. When Edison swam to join her, he noticed an elder guardian behind her.

"Watch out!" he called to Anna, but it was too late. The elder guardian had aimed its laser at her, and she was unaware that it was turning from purple to yellow. The laser from the elder guardian was even more potent than a guardian's attack. Before Anna had a chance to escape the effects of the laser, she was struck with mining fatigue. She couldn't move and didn't have energy to pick a potion from her inventory to help her combat this affliction. Her hearts were incredibly low, and she knew if she didn't swim away quickly, she'd be destroyed.

"Help!" Anna tried to call out, but her voice was weak, and she wasn't sure Edison heard her.

Edison shot as many arrows as he could at the elder guardian, trying to destroy it before it attacked Anna again, but it was pointless. Anna was too weak to move, and the elder guardian was gearing up to strike Anna with another laser. The one-eyed guardian focused its eye on helpless Anna, and it unleashed another powerful laser at her. This time the laser didn't diminish Anna's hearts—it destroyed her.

"Anna!" Edison cried out, but she was gone, and he was left alone to battle the school of guardians swimming toward him as well as a slightly weakened elder guardian. He aimed his arrow at the powerful one-eyed fish, and he knew it was going to be a tough battle.

Two guardians shot lasers at Edison while be battled the elder guardian. His arrow hit the side of the Elder Guardian's scaly body, and the blocky fish was destroyed. Edison swam away from the purple lasers and picked up the raw fish the elder guardian had dropped. He knew Puddles was going to be very happy feasting on all of this fish.

He swam into the ocean monument, past the pillars. Sea lanterns that emitted enough light to guide Edison through the spacious structure lit building. He wanted to explore the chambers inside, but as he searched through the first chamber, he started to feel incredibly weak. From the corner of his eye, he could see another elder guardian.

"Mining fatigue," he said softly, fearful that his last heart was destroyed. He barely had enough energy to pull a bottle of milk from his inventory and take a sip, but he knew that would be the only way to stay in the ocean monument. He didn't have any more potion of Water Breathing left, and he wouldn't be able to return to the ocean without brewing some potion. He used all of the energy he had to grab the milk. He took a sip.

He swam toward a chest, but the elder guardian focused his laser on him and he wasn't able to swim fast enough to escape the powerful and potent ray. His hearts were depleting, and he couldn't swim. He took one last look around the ocean monument, searching for any clues.

Before he faded and awoke in his bed, he spotted

a chest with books. They looked like Amira's journal. He wanted to swim toward them, but he couldn't move.

11

BACK ON LAND

Puddles meowed and Edison pulled the fish from his inventory and fed the cat. It was night, and as Puddles feasted, Edison paced the length of his bedroom, wondering if he should try to teleport to Anna's house or if he should try to get some sleep. He didn't know what to do. He wanted to get back to Anna and tell her about the books he spotted in the ocean monument. He also didn't know if the books actually meant anything. He hadn't gotten close enough to the chest filled with books to inspect it. It could have been a chest filled with enchanted books, or it could be a chest stacked with journals that might provide them with answers.

Edison decided to brew potions. This was something he usually did when he couldn't sleep. He pulled the pufferfish from his inventory and brewed a fresh batch of Water Breathing potion. When he was almost finished, his eyes began to close. He was exhausted. Edison could barely stay awake as he bottled the potion. When he placed the potion in his case, his door began to rattle.

A zombie ripped the door from its hinges, and another zombie was right behind. He quickly put on his diamond armor and sipped a potion to regain his strength. He heard a voice call out, "Help me!" It was familiar, and it startled Edison. He slammed his diamond sword into the two vacant-eyed zombies that crowded the entrance to his home and then doused the undead beasts with potions until they were destroyed. He pocketed the rotten flesh that dropped to the ground and then raced toward the sound of the voice. A voice he couldn't believe he was hearing.

"Billy!" Edison screamed in the pitch-black night. He pulled a torch from his inventory to guide him, but it was very dark, and he could barely see an inch in front of him. An arrow pierced his chest and he lost a heart. He could hear the *click-clang* of skeletons marching in the distance, and Edison knew he was under attack. He could barely see, but he could smell the awful odor emanating from another zombie in front of him. Edison fumbled as he thrust his sword at the beast, hoping he could slice into the oozing flesh and destroy the already dead tormentor.

"Don't worry. I can help," Peyton said as she raced from her home and into the thick of the zombie-and-skeleton battle.

"I'm trying to find Billy." Edison could barely get

the words out. He was out of breath battling the zombie while trying to dodge a sea of arrows.

"I didn't see Billy," Peyton replied as she slammed her sword against the zombie's smelly chest and destroyed it and then raced toward the skeletons. She singlehandedly obliterated them with potions and her sword.

The sun was coming up, and Edison could see Erin rushing toward them. She smiled when the first rays of sunlight landed on the bones and gooey flesh of all of the hostile creatures and they disappeared. "What a way to start the day," she said.

"Let's get breakfast," said Peyton. "Edison, do you want to have breakfast with us?"

Edison blurted out, "Billy, Omar, and Amira are missing! They were trapped underneath a crater in Verdant Valley."

"Slow down," Peyton said. "Are they missing or trapped?"

Tears streamed down Edison's face. "I don't know, but I have to help them."

"You're going to have to tell us what's going on," said Erin.

"Can we talk on the way to Verdant Valley?" asked Edison. He wanted to get back to Anna.

"Yes, of course," Erin said as the two friends accompanied Edison toward the neighboring town.

They walked past the spot where he usually sold his potions, but it was empty. The word must have spread that he wasn't working. As they ran to the lush biome of Verdant Valley, Edison explained everything. By the time they knocked on Anna's door, they knew all the information they needed to help.

Anna opened the door, "Thankfully you're okay! Did you find anything in the ocean?"

Edison told her about the books. "I think we should go back to there. I brewed more water breathing potion."

Peyton and Erin wanted to see the crater. "Can we do that first?" asked Peyton. "Maybe there is something that you might have missed."

The four friends walked to the large patch of land where Dante had commissioned his grand castle to be built, but when they arrived the crater was gone. It had been filled in and covered with grass.

"This is what it looked like before any of the construction started." Anna walked along the grass. "How did someone refill the entire crater? It was enormous."

Edison had no idea, but he heard a voice again in the distance. "Did you guys hear that?"

"Hear what?" asked Peyton.

"It was a voice," said Edison. "It was very muffled, but I thought it sounded like Billy."

"What did the voice say?" asked Anna.

"I couldn't hear," said Edison, "but last night I thought I heard Billy calling for help during the battle with the zombies and the skeletons."

"I thought I heard him too," said Erin, "that's why I ran out of my house."

Edison wondered if Billy had been able to escape

last night but was caught and returned to wherever they were being trapped. He wanted to find Dante and question him. He had to be behind all of this. He also found it very suspicious that Dante's ship had disappeared.

Anna said, "I think I just heard a noise. It didn't sound like a voice, but like someone banging."

Peyton also heard the banging noise and walked toward a large tree overflowing with leaves. "It sounded like it was coming from over here."

The gang followed Peyton toward the tree when Edison stopped.

"What's wrong?" asked Anna.

Edison heard the sound again. He couldn't decipher any words, but it sounded like a cry. "Did you hear that?"

"No," Anna said, "Can we just stand still for a minute and not talk? Maybe if we do, we can hear all of the sounds people keep talking about."

It seemed like an eternity as they stood there waiting for another sound that never came. The silence was broken when they heard a loud voice call out to them.

"Edison!" the voice hollered. "Over here!"

Edison was startled when he turned around to see Dante, dressed in his orange cloak, walking toward them.

12

SPIDERS AND TUNNELS

"You're back?" asked Edison.

"What's going on here?" Dante raced past Edison and toward the patch where the castle was going to be built. "I thought they had started working on the castle. It looks like they haven't begun. I bet they're spending all of their time fixing Amira's boat. This isn't what I expected. I am very disappointed with them."

Edison wondered if Dante was putting on an act. He had to have known what happened. He stood next to Dante. "They had a large crater and they were about to start on the foundation when there was a rumbling underneath the ground."

"A rumbling?" Dante asked. "I've never heard of such a thing. What are you talking about?"

Anna explained, "It was like a mini-earthquake. The ground opened up, and our friends are now missing."

"If this is true, where is the crater? Why isn't the ground shaking now? Why did it stop?" Dante walked around looking for a hole in the ground. "This sounds like nonsense to me."

"It's true," Anna pleaded. "I almost got sucked in to the hole."

"Me too," said Edison.

"I'm sorry to hear that, but I need to go find Omar and Amira. I'm sure they're working on her boat. I will go find them there." Dante bolted off toward the shore.

The gang stayed behind and tried to understand what had just happened. Edison said, "Dante doesn't believe us."

Anna said, "But the more important question is do we believe him?"

Peyton said, "I don't think he was pretending. I really do believe he doesn't know what happened."

"That's so strange," said Anna.

Edison heard the noise again. This time the others heard it too. Peyton said, "We have to find out where it's coming from."

Erin ran over to another large tree. "I hear it better over here. It's much louder."

The sounds were like a muffled voice calling the word *help* and some banging.

"We have to find them. They must be trapped under the ground," said Peyton.

Anna said, "I know how we can get underneath the ground. There is an old home here that was abandoned that has an incredible mineshaft. We also use it to go mining. I bet if we go down there we can get underneath here, or we can at least use our pickaxes to get over here."

They followed Anna to a creepy old Victorian house. She told them about the owner and how he left to live in the jungle. Before the owner moved, he told everyone they could use his mineshaft. Anna told them that although the house was abandoned and appeared creepy, it wasn't scary at all—just neglected.

The door creaked as they opened it. The dark home was a breeding ground for hostile mobs. A skeleton was in the living room and aimed a bow and arrow at them. The arrow struck Edison's unarmored arm.

Anna leapt at the skeleton and hit the bony beast with her enchanted diamond sword, destroying it with one blow.

"Good job," Edison commended her.

Anna traded her diamond sword in for a torch. She clutched the torch, which provided them with a small light on the dark stairway.

"You guys are going to have to protect me because I can't carry a sword and the torch," she said as she led them down what seemed like a never-ending flight of stairs.

When they reached the bottom of the stairs, a pair of red eyes glared at them. "Cave spider," Anna called out, and Edison jumped toward the spider, sliced into its body, and obliterated it.

Anna placed the torch on the wall and pulled out her diamond sword. "We have to be very careful down here. It's not an easy place to mine. There are always hostile mobs here."

The group walked slowly, keeping a lookout for hostile mobs that might spawn in the dark, musty abandoned mineshaft. An old mine cart was on a track in the mine. Edison peered inside, and a cave spider lunged at him. He swiftly hit the spider.

Anna stopped. "I hear them. Do you guys?"

There were sounds of voices.

"Yes, there is definitely somebody down here," said Edison.

The gang rushed toward the sound of the voices, but they stopped when four skeletons spawned in front of them, shooting a barrage of arrows in their direction.

Edison sprinted toward the skeletons and splashed them with potions to weaken them. Anna, Peyton, and Erin slammed their swords into the skeletons. The sounds of clanging bones were deafening as they battled the beasts in the mineshaft. When the final skeleton was destroyed, the gang raced toward the spot where they had heard the voices, but there was no sound.

"Do you hear anything?" asked Edison.

Peyton put her ear against the dirt wall. "No."

A silverfish crawled past Edison's feet, and he swung his diamond sword at the pesky insect. It was then when he heard a noise. It was a faint sound, but he could hear it.

Someone was calling for help.

13

SOUNDS

Edison took out his pickaxe and banged it against the blocky dirt wall, but he couldn't get to the other side.

"It's a really thick wall," Anna said as she pounded the pickaxe against the dirt.

"This is harder than we thought," said Peyton.

Erin spotted a green creeper walking toward them. The explosive mob was inches from Peyton. Erin screamed, "Peyton, turn around!"

Peyton moved and the creeper exploded, destroying her. Erin's voice cracked as she questioned, "What should we do? Should we go back and get Peyton in Farmer's Bay?"

Anna responded while banging her pickaxe against the wall, "We can't go back to Farmer's Bay. She should TP to us."

The trio used all of their strength to reach the other side of the wall, but they weren't even making a dent.

Edison was exhausted. "This could take forever." He paused and grabbed some milk from his inventory. He had to replenish his energy supply.

"What if we can't do this?" asked Erin.

"We can't give up." Anna looked over at Edison. "We have to save our friends."

"I know." Edison continued hitting the pickaxe into the wall.

A voice called out, "Help!"

Edison put down his pickaxe down and screamed, "Billy? Can you hear us?"

"Yes," the faint voice replied.

"We're coming to help you," said Edison.

The gang worked as fast as they could, and soon there was a small hole the size of a brick in the wall. Edison could see Billy's eyes peering through. Billy said, "We're stuck down here, and our inventories are almost empty. We're starving."

"I have an idea," Edison said as he passed potions through the hole in the wall. "You guys take these. Once you've regained your energy, you can use the strength to break through the wall. If we all work together, we can get the wall torn down sooner."

With people working to knock down the wall on both sides, they were able to make a larger hole. Billy was the first to climb through to Edison, and Amira and Omar followed behind him.

"Who trapped you?" asked Edison.

"We don't know," Omar explained. "We all fell into the ground when we were working on the castle. We were trapped in a small room, but there wasn't anybody there."

Anna said, "We have to get out of here. I don't like staying down in the mineshaft for too long. There are many hostile mobs, and it's not safe here."

The group hurried through the mineshaft back into the old Victorian home and into the grassy open spaces outside it. Omar looked out at the area where the crater had been. "What happened? Where's the crater?"

"Someone must have filled it in," said Anna. "We are trying to find out who that is."

"We have quite a mystery to solve," said Edison. "I'm hoping we could all work together to solve it."

Peyton rushed toward them. "You're out! That's fantastic!"

Edison delivered the bad news. They didn't know who was behind all of this, and they weren't any closer to finding out. As he spoke, a thunderous boom shook the trees, and Edison looked down to make sure the ground wasn't opening. He was relieved to realize it was just a rainstorm.

Anna suggested everyone heading to her house to get shelter from the rain. While they ran toward the safety of Anna's house, an army of skeletons spawned by her front door. Brushing the rain from their eyes, the gang grabbed their armor and diamond swords, ready to battle the bony battalion. Arrows flew through the wet sky as raindrops formed puddles on the ground. Each step they took toward the skeletons splashed.

Edison didn't have time to pull a potion from his inventory. Four skeletons surrounded him, and although he tried to maneuver the sword to strike as many skeletons as he could, he wasn't very successful. He was losing hearts as the rain pounded on his helmeted head. Another thunderous boom shook Verdant Valley as more skeletons spawned, and Edison was outnumbered. Before he could strike another skeleton, an arrow landed on his arm, and he lost his final heart. He respawned in his bed.

Rain was hitting his window, and a zombie was ripping his door from its hinges. Puddles meowed to announce the zombie's entrance into the center of Edison's living room.

Edison grabbed a handful of potion from the brewing station and splashed it on the undead beast. Then he sliced through the zombie and picked up the rotten flesh the zombie dropped when it was destroyed. Even though the zombie was gone, his living room still had a faint smell of the creature's horrid odor. Edison held his nose as he sprinted into the rainy afternoon to look for his friends.

"Edison," Billy called out. "Over here! Help!"

Edison spotted Billy in the middle of a battle, but it wasn't with a hostile mob. It was with Dante.

14

ON THE BOAT

Edison rushed toward Dante, but Billy struck him with his sword and he disappeared.

"We have to go to the boat," said Billy. "He must have respawned there."

As they sprinted to the shoreline, four zombies lumbered down the sandy path. Edison pierced a zombie's flesh with the diamond sword, infuriating the other three zombies. They grabbed at Edison, depleting his hearts and destroying him. The zombies were too much to battle alone, and Edison respawned in his bed again. Puddles meowed at him.

Edison could see the sun through the window—the rain had stopped. He bolted from his home to meet Billy. When he walked into Billy's living room, he was surprised to find Anna there.

"Billy told me all about Dante," Anna said. "We have to go see him."

Edison only saw Billy and Dante fight. He didn't know what had happened before the fight began, and he wanted to find out. As they rushed toward the yacht, Billy explained how Dante had lunged at him and begun to fight. They'd exchanged no words exchanged, and he had no idea what provoked the attack. He had to see Dante and find out what was happening.

The trio climbed up the ladder and onto Dante's lavish ship. Gregson appeared. "Can I help you?"

"We want to see Dante," said Billy.

"Dante isn't here. He won't be back for a rather long time. Why don't you come back later?" said Gregson. He pointed to the ladder.

"Where is he?" asked Billy.

"It's none of your business," replied Gregson. "In fact he might never come back."

"Really?" asked Anna. "He's just going to leave his ship here?"

"That's a possibility," Gregson responded vaguely. "And why would I give you guys information? I don't know you guys. I've never seen you before."

Edison knew Gregson. He had met him a few times, and the butler's statement—*I've never seen you before*—struck Edison as quite strange. He wanted to question Gregson, but before he could speak, he heard voices coming from below.

"Is someone here?" asked Anna.

"Again, that's none of your business. You're strangers." Gregson was annoyed and tried to lead them to the ladder so they could exit the boat.

The voices grew louder, and Edison thought they sounded like screams. "I'm sorry, but it sounds like someone is in trouble. I can't leave this boat without finding out what's happening."

"Do I have to repeat myself for the millionth time?" Gregson raised his voice. "What happens on this ship is none of your business."

"If someone is in trouble, then it's everyone's business," Edison proclaimed. He took out his enchanted diamond sword and waved it at Gregson.

"Please put that sword down," said Gregson quite calmly.

"If you let us see what's going on below deck," said Edison.

The screams grew louder. Anna said, "It sounds like Amira. We have to go find out what's going on."

Edison pushed Gregson out of the way, and he stormed down the stairs with Anna and Billy by his side. They raced down a long corridor with many doors, opening each to try to find the people who were screaming for help.

"This way," said Anna as she led them toward a door at the end of the hall. She tried to open the door, but it was locked.

Anna and Edison traded in their pickaxes for swords as they broke down the door. Billy stood behind them with his sword out, ready to attack anyone who stopped them from helping the people trapped behind the door. Gregson rushed down, carrying potions in both hands. He splashed them on Billy as Billy slammed his sword into Gregson's tuxedo-clad, unarmored body. The potions weakened Billy, and he barely had enough strength to strike Gregson again. He used his last bit of energy to hit Gregson's arm, which cost the butler his final heart. He disappeared.

Billy was wobbly and tried to trade his sword for a pickaxe, but he couldn't muster up enough strength to put the sword away or pull a potion from his inventory. He needed to regain his strength. He took a deep breath and gathered every bit of energy he had to pull out the bottle of potion he desperately needed.

Anna and Edison couldn't help Billy; they were almost done tearing down the door. The yells grew even louder, and they could make out Amira's and Omar's voices. When they finally tore down the door, Amira rushed out, followed by Omar and two unknown people. One was a man in jeans, a black shirt, and a blue helmet ran out, and the other was wearing dirty white pants. Both strangers thanked them for helping them escape.

"I thought I was never going to get out of here," said Omar.

"Anna! Edison! Billy! Help me! We have to get off this boat," screamed Amira.

"I am forever grateful to you," said the man in the jeans.

"You're safe now," Anna smiled.

"Who is this?" asked Billy as he gulped a potion to regain his strength after the battle.

"This is Dante," Amira replied.

Dante looked at the man in the stained white pants. "And this is Gregson."

Gregson looked at his pants, "I'm sorry for looking so disheveled, but someone stole my skin."

15

IN THE BOOKS

"**W**hat?" asked Edison. "How are they Dante and Gregson?"

Amira started to talk, "Someone—" But her words were cut off when a loud explosion rocked the boat. The gang fell to the ground. The boat began to tilt to one side. Edison grabbed onto the wall to avoid falling off. The ship sank into the water, and within seconds they were submerged. Edison swam to shore, but he didn't see any of his friends. Panicked, he raced back into the ocean to search for them. The water was up to his knees, and he wanted to look below the surface but he didn't have a potion of Water Breathing on him. He had left it in his chest. He slowly walked back to the shore and waited, but nobody showed up. After he waited for a bit, the sky grew dark, and Edison knew he had to return home.

On the path, two block-carrying Endermen walked

past. The lanky creatures locked eyes with Edison and began to shriek, and he knew the only way he'd survive was by sprinting back to the water. The water was fatal to the Endermen, and when they followed Edison into the water, they were destroyed. Walking out of the water, Edison heard someone call out to him. He turned around.

Amira swam toward him. When Amira reached him, she said, "Take this," and handed Edison a potion of Water Breathing. They both took a sip and went deep underneath the sea.

"Where are we going?" asked Edison.

"I have to show you something," said Amira.

Edison followed Amira, but he stopped when he spotted an elder guardian swimming in his direction. He tried to escape the one-eyed fish, but it was impossible. The fish focused its eye on him and unleashed a laser. The powerful laser paralyzed him with mining fatigue.

"Come on!" Amira said to Edison without looking back.

Edison didn't have the energy to respond, but Amira turned around when she didn't see him swim toward her.

"Edison!" she cried, racing toward the elder guardian, swiping the spiky fish with her diamond sword until it was destroyed.

The mining fatigue faded, and Edison was able to grab a potion from his inventory while Amira swam toward him. She handed him the raw fish the elder guardian had dropped. "Take this for Puddles."

Edison smiled. "Thanks."

"No time to thank me, but you have to follow me. I have something important to show you." She swam very quickly, and Edison had a hard time keeping up with her.

He almost lost her when she swiftly swam past a pillar, but he caught up as she swam into the first chamber. The room was familiar. It was the place with the chest filled with books. Amira swam to the chest and lifted up the first book from the chest. She opened it and started to read aloud.

"The seas were rough today, but I was happy I could loot many ships. There are two ships I've seen during my travels. One a large yacht, and another is a replica of a pirate ship. I would like to loot the contents of these ships."

Edison listened while he kept an eye at the entrance. He was worried another elder guardian would swim into the dimly lit chamber. The faint light from the sea lantern wasn't powerful enough to light up the entire room, and Edison worried he wouldn't see an elder guardian until it was too late.

He swam to Amira and picked up one of the books from the chest, "Who wrote this?"

"The person who stole Dante's skin," Amira explained. "His name is Jace. He's a pirate that terrorizes people at sea."

She read another passage. "When I have successfully looted all of the boats in the Overworld, I will be the wealthiest person in the biome."

"Wow, I wonder how long Jace has been doing this," said Edison as he stared at the numerous volumes.

"For years. I always thought Jace was a made-up story, but he wasn't. We have to stop him before he hurts anyone else."

"Do you think he was the one who caused the crater to open and then disappear?" asked Edison.

"Yes, I think he's responsible for everything," Amira replied as she placed the books in her inventory. But her inventory was almost full. "Can you take some of these books? I don't have room for all of them, and I need them to see what he has stolen from other people so I can hand it back to them. It looks like he kept a pretty good log of all the loot he stole."

"Wow." Edison looked through one of the books before placing it in his inventory. It listed all of the items Jace had taken from a boat he had robbed a few weeks ago. The list included potions, swords, and a diamond helmet. Edison thought about the person who had lost all of those items and how happy they would be if Amira returned it to them.

Edison was too distracted with the book to notice the elder guardian that focused its eye on him. The purple laser was already changing color before Edison had a chance to escape. He had mining fatigue and was frozen as he watched the elder guardian destroy Amira. He was too weak to fight back, and within seconds he was destroyed. He awoke in his bed. As he stood up, he almost fell over in shock when he saw a man in an orange cloak pointing a sword at him.

"You're not Dante?" Edison wasn't sure why he bothered to ask that question when he already knew the answer.

16

PIRATE'S LIFE

"**Y**ou're coming with me!" Jace swung his diamond sword at Edison, slicing into Edison's arm and depleting one of his hearts.

Edison's energy was low, and he wasn't wearing armor—he had no other choice but to follow Jace. The man walked behind Edison, pointed his sword at Edison's back, and instructed him to travel to the shore.

"You're my prisoner now, so you better listen." Jace pushed the sword into Edison's back and pulled it out. The pain radiated down his spine, but he didn't cry. He didn't want Jace to know how much it hurt. He was down to two hearts, and it was getting dark. He knew if one hostile mob spawned in their path, he would be destroyed. He felt weak as Jace led him to the shore.

When they reached the sandy beach of Farmer's Bay, Edison gasped. Docked at the shore was one of the largest pirate ships he'd ever seen. The boat was massive, and Edison couldn't believe something that size could be seaworthy. It was three times the size of Dante's yacht. Edison assumed all of the treasures Jace had stolen were stored on the boat. It was so large Jace could have kept endless treasures on the ship.

When they finally reached the boat, Jace stood next to Edison and pointed to the ladder hanging off the side of the ship.

"Get on the boat," instructed Jace.

Edison looked up and couldn't even see the top. The black pirate ship was so tall that it seemed to reach the sky.

"Do I have to repeat myself? Climb aboard," Jace ordered Edison.

Edison didn't listen. He stood by the side of the ship and refused to climb aboard.

"You're making me very angry." Jace raised his voice. "Climb aboard or I will put everyone on Hardcore mode and then destroy your friends."

Edison listened, and he began to carefully climb up the stairs. It felt like an eternity before he reached the top of the ladder and climbed onto the ship.

The pirate that had stolen Gregson's skin stood on top of the ship and asked Jace what he should do with Edison. "Should I put him with the others?" he asked.

Edison wondered who the others were. He hoped it was his friends, because he missed them and wanted to be reunited with them.

"Of course," Jace responded while he nodded his head.

"This way," said Jace's accomplice. The man led Edison down a massive hallway. Edison listened for his friend's voices, but it was silent. The fake butler opened a door and threw Edison into a dark room. A pair of red eyes stared at him from the corner of the room. Edison took out his diamond sword and slammed it against the spider. Once the spider was destroyed, Edison was alone. He wondered where the others were and if he could find them. His energy was still quite low, and he pulled an apple from his inventory and began to eat. As he chewed, Anna spawned in front of him.

"What?" questioned Edison.

Anna placed her finger in front of her red lips, "*Shh!* You have to be quiet. We don't want him to hear us."

Billy spawned next to Edison. Edison tried not to speak, but it seemed like an impossible request. He wanted to talk to his friends. Omar spawned in the center of the room. Edison was shocked when he saw Amira spawn next to Omar. Then Dante and Gregson appeared.

Anna said in a whisper that was so soft and quiet that Edison wasn't sure he could hear her correctly, "We were all here the entire time. You had no idea we were here, right?"

"Not at all," said Edison. "Why were you trying to trick me?"

"We weren't trying to trick you," explained Anna. "We want to trick Jace."

Omar said, "When we hear Jace or his friend's footsteps, we're all going to take a potion of Invisibility, and then he'll think we all escaped."

Amira added. "And that's when we attack him."

"We're ready to take him down," said Billy, "but we need you to give us some more potion. We need three bottles."

"Once we all have the potions, we can capture Jace, and there will be justice. I can travel around the world with Omar returning all of the stolen goods," proclaimed Amira.

"You're leaving Farmer's Bay?" Edison asked Omar.

"Just for a little bit. I said I'd help Amira. However, I don't want to leave until the castle is completed," said Omar.

This comment irritated Amira, and they began to bicker until Anna told them to be quiet. "We can't fight with each other. We have to be quiet and stick to the plan."

"If you'd like," suggested Dante, "Gregson and I could deliver half of the stolen goods back to the owners, which will lighten your responsibilities, and Omar can stay here and finish the castle."

Amira and Omar liked that plan. Omar said, "Now I can stay in Farmer's Bay. I'm not like you Amira. I'm not cut out for a life at sea."

"I understand," said Amira, "It's not for everybody."

"Okay, now that we have that settled," said Anna, "We have to get back to the original plan." She looked over at Edison and asked him, "Edison, do you have any bottles of the potion of Invisibility?"

"We need them, because this plan is fantastic," added Billy.

Edison agreed this sounded like a fantastic plan, but there was only one problem: Edison didn't have any bottles of the potion of Invisibility. They heard footsteps in the distance. They had to come up with another plan, and they had to do it fast.

17

POWER OF POTIONS

"I don't have any bottles of the potion of Invisibility," Edison told them.

"What are we going to do?" asked Billy.

The footsteps grew louder, and they knew they were in a race against time. They needed another plan.

"I have an idea," said Anna. "I have three bottles. How about Omar, Amira, and I take them, but we leave Billy, Edison, Dante, and Gregson visible. When Jace or his evil sidekick come inside you can tell them we escaped. As you distract them with the story, we'll attack them and capture them." She spoke quickly, trying to explain all of the details of the plan before Jace or his accomplice opened the door.

"I guess so," said Edison. "It's our only hope."

Anna, Omar, and Amira gulped the potion and disappeared in seconds. The door opened, and before Edison, Billy, Dante, or Gregson could speak, Jace screamed, "Where are the others? There are supposed to be three other people in here."

"They escaped," explained Dante.

"Escaped how?" Jace walked to the wall, inspecting it for any holes. "That's impossible."

"It sure is," said Anna as she splashed a potion on Jace, weakening him. Billy struck Jace with his sword.

"Stop!" Jace screamed as his hearts depleted.

Edison put on his armor and lunged at Jace with his diamond sword. "Now you're trapped."

Amira's potion of Invisibility wore off, and she pulled one of Jace's journals from her inventory. "Do you see what we've found? We have all of your journals. We know everyone you have stolen from. Now we're going to go through your boat and return all of the stolen treasure."

Dante said, "Before we do that, I want my skin back."

"No," Jace's voice was weak.

Dante said, "That wasn't a question, it was an order. I want my skin back."

"So do I," added Gregson.

Jace's sidekick rushed into the room. "What's going on, Jace?" he asked.

Gregson jumped at the man dressed in a tuxedo. "I want my skin back too. That's my bowtie."

Jace's sidekick shed the skin, and Gregson was reunited with his formal attire. Now the sidekick wore the stained jeans. Gregson pointed his diamond sword at the sidekick. "Stand next to Jace."

Amira said, "You guys blew up my boat."

"We had to," explained Jace. "I knew you found one of my journals. It was just a matter of time before you found me."

"Why did you destroy all of the work I did on the castle?" asked Omar.

"I thought there was treasure below it, but—" said Jace.

"There wasn't," said Anna. "Why are you such a troublemaker? Why can't you just leave people alone?"

Jace had no reply.

"We are going to keep you prisoner on this boat," said Dante. "Gregson and I will travel around the seas of the Overworld, and you will accompany us as we return the treasure. You will be the crew on our boat and will help us maintain it."

Gregson added, "You will also help clean it."

"That's your job," said Dante.

"Not anymore." Gregson smiled.

Amira and Edison handed Dante and Gregson the stack of books they had taken from the ocean monument. "Here are all of the journals. They name all of the treasures and the people who had their items stolen."

"Thank you," said Dante. "When we return to see the castle, we will tell you about all of the people we have seen and about their reactions when they are reunited with their stolen treasures."

Amira said, "I can't wait to hear about it."

Omar smiled. "We have a lot of work to do."

"We can help you guys," suggested Anna.

"Great, we can use all the help we can get," said Omar.

Dante looked over at Jace and then pointed to the jeans he wore. "I still don't have my skin back."

Jace reluctantly gave Dante back his skin. "You're not going to get away with this."

"Me?" Dante was shocked. "I am trying to give people back items that you stole from them. I have the entire Overworld on my side. You're the one who is not going to get away with this."

"Watch them," Amira said to Dante and Gregson as she looked at Jace and his friend. "They are tricky. You have to make sure they don't escape."

"We will watch them. Now that the world knows about them—that they are real and not just a tale people tell on the seas—they won't have any power," Gregson assured Amira.

"We'll see you when the castle is complete," said Dante.

The gang left the pirate ship and headed straight to Verdant Valley to make Dante's castle.

18

THE CASTLE

"I have great news." Edison rushed toward Omar and Amira.

"So do we," Amira said as she placed the final brick on the castle.

"Wow," Edison marveled. "This is stunning. You guys did an amazing job," Edison walked on the bridge, over the moat, and into the grand castle.

Anna was helping decorate the great room in the castle. As she placed an emerald design on the wall, she said, "What do you think?"

"This is the amazing. Has Billy seen it?" asked Edison.

"Did somebody call out my name?" asked Billy. He walked over to Edison, "You have to see the grounds. I crafted a large garden for the castle. I even made an enormous maze. I want to see if you can get through it without getting lost."

Edison was apologetic. "I wish I could have helped you with the castle."

"You helped us find Jace," said Amira. "You were helpful."

"You have to run your potion stand. I feel badly that I couldn't help you with the crowds," said Billy.

"What's your good news?" asked Omar.

"I was asked to take part in a brewing competition." He showed them the letter. It was taking place in a month, and he had to practice before the big day.

"That's incredible," exclaimed Amira.

Peyton and Erin rushed toward the castle, and they shouted in unison, "Guys, the large pirate ship is back."

Dante and Gregson walked into Verdant Valley with Jace and his sidekick, who had their heads down as they walked behind.

"This is the most amazing castle in the Overworld. You guys did the best job," exclaimed Dante.

"We're so happy you like it," Omar said.

"Like it? We love it," Dante said.

"Do you want a tour?" asked Amira. "Once we get an okay from you, Omar and I are going to start repairing my boat. I can't wait to get back to sea."

As they took a tour of the castle, Dante told them, "I think I want to stay on land for a while. We've delivered most of the treasure. I'm going to live in the castle." He looked at Amira, "Instead of fixing your boat, I'd like to give you my boat. You can use it to return the remaining treasure."

"Really?" Amira couldn't believe her ears. "You're

going to give me the boat? That's amazing." Then she stopped and her eyes began to tear up.

Omar asked, "What's wrong?"

"I spent so much time being alone, I forgot what it's like to have people around. I'm going to miss all of you." Amira's tears rolled down her face.

"I'd love to go with you for a little while. I've never traveled on the sea," said Omar.

"That would be fantastic," Amira smiled.

When the group finished the tour of the castle, they walked Amira and Omar to the shore to say goodbye.

Omar promised Edison, "I will only be gone for a month. I will be back to see you in the brewing competition."

"That's great," said Edison. "I can't wait to see you there."

"Me too," said Omar.

As they all said goodbye to their friends, Dante said, "Before you go, can we have one big party at the castle?"

"That sounds great!" said Amira.

The gang ran back to Verdant Valley for the first of many parties at the castle. The sun set as they feasted on cake and cookies before nightfall.

The End

WANT MORE OF STEVIE AND HIS FRIENDS?

Read the Unofficial Overworld Adventure series!

Escape from the
Overworld
DANICA DAVIDSON

Attack on the
Overworld
DANICA DAVIDSON

The Rise of
Herobrine
DANICA DAVIDSON

Down into the
Nether
DANICA DAVIDSON

The Armies of
Herobrine
DANICA DAVIDSON

Battle with the
Wither
DANICA DAVIDSON

Available wherever books are sold!

DO YOU LIKE FICTION FOR MINECRAFTERS?

Read the
Unofficial Minecrafters Academy series!

Zombie Invasion
WINTER MORGAN

Skeleton Battle
WINTER MORGAN

Battle in the Overworld
WINTER MORGAN

Attack on Minecrafters Academy
WINTER MORGAN

Hidden in the Chest
WINTER MORGAN

Encounters in End City
WINTER MORGAN

Available wherever books are sold!